ATSUKO MOROZUMI

The Wild Swans

HANS CHRISTIAN ANDERSEN

RETOLD BY MATHEW PRICE

MATHEW PRICE LIMITED

This edition first published 2003 by Mathew Price Limited
The Old Glove Factory, Bristol Road, Sherborne, Dorset DT9 4HP, UK
Text copyright © Mathew Price 2003
Illustrations copyright © Atsuko Morozumi 1996, 2003

ISBN 1-84248-073-1

Designed by Douglas Martin
Printed in China

ONCE UPON A TIME there was a princess
called Elisa, who had eleven brothers.
They lived very happily in a beautiful palace until
the day their father married a wicked queen.

While the whole palace was celebrating the royal wedding, the queen gave the children sand in a tea cup and told them to pretend it was something delicious.

Then the very next week the queen sent Elisa to the country to live with a peasant family. As for the princes, she soon poisoned the king's mind against them.

Then she cast a spell upon them.

"Fly out into the world and fend for yourselves," she cried, and the brothers were changed into beautiful white swans.

With a strange call they flew out of the palace windows, across the park and over the forest.

For many years Elisa lived in the peasants' cottage. She had no toys but she made a hole in a leaf and peeped through it at the sun. She imagined she could see her brothers' eyes on her and feel their kisses on her cheeks.

When she was fifteen, Elisa returned to the palace. The queen saw how sweet and pretty she was and she hated her for it. She could not turn her into a swan because the king wanted to see her, so she gave her a bath with three enchanted toads to make her mean and ugly.

But Elisa never noticed them and when she stood up there were just three red poppies floating on the water.

Then the queen stained her body with walnut juice and smeared her face and hair with stinking ointment.

When the king saw her he was shocked and said she was no daughter of his.

Elisa slipped sadly out of the palace. She walked all day, till she came to the great forest. She heard water splashing in a pool and washed her face there until her skin shone clear again.

Then she wandered deeper into the forest. It grew quieter and quieter until she could hear her footsteps on the moss.

At last she lay down to sleep. She was very lonely but she was determined to find her brothers again.

Next day Elisa met an old woman, who gave her some berries. She said she had seen eleven swans with golden crowns, swimming in the brook and showed Elisa where a stream ran down past steep cliffs to the sea.

On the beach were eleven white feathers.

Just before sunset eleven swans landed nearby. As the sun dipped below the sea, they changed into eleven handsome princes. Elisa rushed towards them, calling out their names. They were overjoyed to see her and told her everything that had happened.

"During the day we are swans," they said. "When the sun sets, we are human. We live two days from here, across the sea. The only land in between is a small rock where we rest for the night. Without it we could never visit our homeland".

"Take me back with you," begged Elisa.

They spent that night weaving a net from willow bark and tough rushes until it was big enough to hold Elisa. When dawn came, the swans took the net in their beaks and flew high up into the clouds.

They flew all day but because they were carrying Elisa, they could not fly as fast as usual. If they could not reach the rock by nightfall they would all fall to their deaths.

As evening drew near, a storm blew up and still Elisa could not see the rock. The swans' wings beat more and more desperately. Lightning flashed and the sky darkened. The sun was just reaching the horizon when the swans plunged downward.

Suddenly Elisa saw a little rock beneath them, sticking up like a seal poking its head above the water.

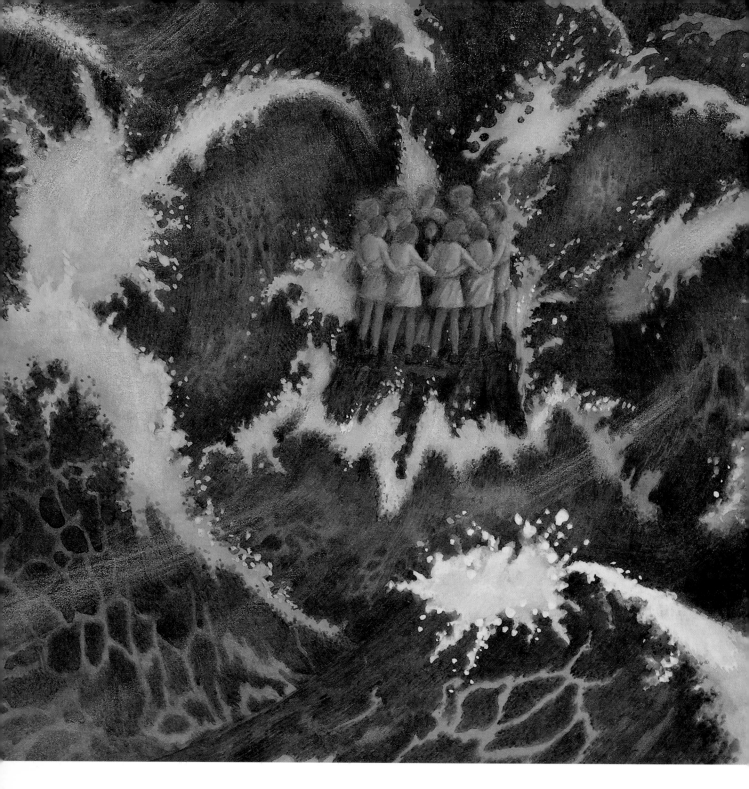

As her foot touched firm ground the sun flickered and was gone. She could see her brothers standing round her, arm in arm. There was only just room enough for all of them.

All night long the thunder crashed and lightning lit up

the sky. The sea burst against the rock, soaking them
to the skin. At last the storm passed and morning came.
As they flew off again, the white foam on the dark
green waves looked like millions of swans, floating on
the water.

They landed by a cave hung with creepers. "This is your bedroom," said her youngest brother. "Sweet dreams."

That night she dreamed of the old woman who had given her berries in the wood.

"Your brothers *can* be freed if you have the courage", said the old woman. "You must knit them shirts from the nettles that grow here and in the churchyard. If you throw them over the swans the spell will be broken. But from now until they are free, you must never speak. One word from you would pierce their hearts like a dagger."

Elisa woke to find a nettle lying beside her.

She started work at once. She had just finished the first shirt when a hunting horn rang out and into the clearing rode a young king. He thought he had never seen a girl so beautiful.

She was brought to the palace and dressed in royal purple and her hair braided with pearls. She looked so lovely that the king married her at once. The bells rang out and the whole country rejoiced. Only the archbishop shook his head and said that she was a witch.

Elisa came to love the young king and longed to tell him everything. Instead each night she secretly knitted shirts out of nettles. When she ran out, she had to go to the churchyard to pick more. A circle of vampires sat on a gravestone but they never touched her. One night the archbishop saw what she was doing and told the king.

The next time she slipped out, they both followed her.

When the king saw Elisa with the vampires, he thought that she must be a witch. "Let the people judge her", he said. And the people judged that she should be burned at the stake.

But still Elisa never spoke. She was taken to a prison cell and instead of silks and velvet they gave her the bundle of nettles for a pillow and the stinging nettle shirts for a blanket. For Elisa this was the best present they could have given her. There was still one more shirt left to do.

The archbishop came to see her but she sent him away and worked all night on the shirt.

An hour before dawn, her brothers arrived at the palace gates and demanded to see the king. But the servants refused to wake him. When at last he came, the sun had risen and eleven swans were flying over the palace.

A large crowd came to see her taken to the stake. They tried to take the nettle shirts as souvenirs but eleven white swans flew down and settled around her on the cart.

As their powerful wings beat back the crowd, Elisa threw the shirts over them, and they became eleven handsome

princes. But the youngest prince still had a swan's wing
for an arm because Elisa had not quite finished the last
shirt. "At last I can speak," said Elisa. "I am not a witch."
 "Yes, she is innocent", said her eldest brother, and he
told the whole story.

The king was really happy because he truly loved Elisa.

Then all the wood packed around the stake took root and burst into flower. As they walked back to the palace, the church bells rang out of their own accord and all the birds came to welcome her home.